THE TIME MACHINE

RETOLD BY PAULINE FRANCIS

Published by Evans Brothers Limited
2A Portman Mansions
Chiltern Street
London W1U 6NR

© Evans Brothers Limited 2002
First published 2002

British Library Cataloguing in Publication data
Francis, Pauline
    The time machine - (Fast Track Classics)
    1. Science fiction 2. Children's stories
    I. Title II. Wells, H. G. (Herbert George), 1866-1946
    823.9'14 [J]

ISBN 0 237 52406 6

VISIT OUR WEBSITE
Evans
www.evansbooks.co.uk

THE TIME MACHINE

Introduction

Herbert George Wells was born in Kent, England, in 1866. His father owned a small shop and his mother was a lady's maid. Wells left school at the age of fourteen, but when he was eighteen years old, he won a scholarship to study science at London University.

By the time he was in his early thirties, Wells had already written the science fiction novels that made him famous: *The Time Machine* (1895), *The Invisible Man* (1897) and *The War of the Worlds* (1898).

The Time Machine tells the story of a Time Traveller who builds his own Time Machine and travels to the world of AD802,701 – a world which appears happy and perfect at first, but hides a terrible secret.

For the last forty years of his life, H.G. Wells was a world-famous writer. He wrote about forty novels and almost thirty non-fiction books, including the well-known *A Short History of the World*. H.G. Wells died in 1946.

CHAPTER ONE

The Time Machine

"I want you to listen to me carefully," our friend said suddenly, as we were having dinner at his house in London. "I have an idea which might seem strange to you." He paused for a moment. "I think it is possible to travel backwards and forwards in time," he said at last.

We all shook our heads in disbelief.

"Why not?" he asked. "We can move backwards and forwards, and up and down, in space. Why shouldn't we move backwards and forwards in time?"

We laughed at his question.

"That's why I didn't tell you until now," he said.

"Until now?" I cried. "Do you mean that you can prove it?"

Our friend – I'll call him the Time Traveller from now on – smiled at us and walked slowly out of the room. We heard his slippers shuffling down the long corridor to his laboratory. Soon afterwards, he came back, holding in his hand something small and metallic – like a clock.

"This is a model of my Time Machine," the Time Traveller said.

We all got up and looked carefully at it.

"Now," the Time Traveller said, "in a moment, I am going to press this lever. Then my machine will vanish into the future. Watch carefully. This is not a trick. You will not see this machine again."

The Time Traveller put out his finger to press the lever, then he stopped. He took hold of the hand of one of his friends.

"Press now!" he said.

We all saw the lever move. I am sure it wasn't a trick. I felt a breath of wind, and the flame in the lamp flickered. One of the candles on the mantelpiece even went out. The little machine turned and became blurred. Then it disappeared.

Everyone was silent.

"Well?" the Time Traveller asked.

"Do you seriously believe that the machine has travelled into time?" the Doctor asked.

"Of course," the Time Traveller answered. "And I have nearly finished a big machine in my laboratory. Then I shall travel myself." He looked at us. "Would you like to see it?" he asked.

The Time Traveller led the way to his laboratory. And there it stood – an ugly thing made of ivory and brass and shimmering quartz – the Time Machine.

"Are you serious?" we asked in amazement. "Or is this another of your tricks?"

The Time Traveller held up the lamp and looked at us.

"On this machine," he said, "I intend to explore time. I was never more serious in my whole life."

I don't think any of us believed in the Time Machine – until the strange events of the following Thursday. I went to have dinner with the Time Traveller as usual. I arrived late and there were already four or five guests there. I looked around for the Time Traveller, but I could not see him. One of the guests, the Doctor, looked at his watch, then at a piece of paper in his hand.

"I want to read you this note from the Time Traveller," he announced.

"If I am not back at seven, go to dinner. I shall explain when I come."

"Perhaps he is time-travelling," I joked.

At eight o' clock, as we were still eating, the dining-room door opened and there stood the Time Traveller. He was in a terrible state. His coat was dusty and dirty, and smeared with green. His hair was untidy and much greyer than the week before. I had never seen such an anxious look on his pale face.

"Good heavens, man!" the Doctor cried. "What's the matter?"

The Time Traveller hesitated, then limped into the room. We stared at him, waiting for him to speak. But he drank a glass of wine, then looked at us in silence.

"What on earth have you been up to, man?" the Doctor asked again.

"I'm all right," the Time Traveller whispered.

He drank another glass of wine. His eyes grew brighter, and a faint colour came into his cheeks. Then he spoke again, as if he was not sure of what he was saying.

"I'm going to wash," he said, "and then I'll explain everything. Save me a bit of that meat."

He put down his glass and walked towards the door. I saw his feet as he went out. He was wearing only a pair of tattered, blood-stained socks.

"I think it's something to do with the Time Machine," I said.

"Don't they have clothes-brushes in the future?" somebody asked, laughing.

When the Time Traveller came back, one of the guests – a newspaper Editor - spoke immediately.

"The story!" he cried. "Tell us the story!"

"Not before I have eaten," the Time Traveller smiled.

"One word," I said. "Have you been time-travelling?"

"Yes," the Time Traveller answered, with his mouth full and nodding his head.

At last the Time Traveller pushed away his plate, and looked round at us.

"I am sorry," he said, "but I was starving. I've had a most amazing time. I will tell you the story of what happened to me, but you must not interrupt. You will think that I am lying. But it's true – every word of it! In the last ten hours, I've lived eight days…such days that no human being has ever lived. I'm very tired, but I shan't sleep until I've told you. No interruptions! Do you agree?"

"Agreed," we all cried.

The Time Traveller began his story. I have written down exactly what he said. But I wish you could see his white face in the bright light of the lamp, and hear the emotions in his voice. At first, we looked at each other as he spoke. Then we looked only at his face.

This is his story…

CHAPTER TWO
Into the future

"I only finished the Time Machine at ten o'clock this morning," the Time Traveller began. "I tightened all the screws one last time and sat inside. I pressed the starting lever, then the stopping lever straight away. I wanted to time travel for a second or two, just to try it out.

For those few seconds, I seemed to spin round and round. I felt as if I was falling, as you do in a dream. This feeling quickly went away and I was able to see my laboratory clearly again. It looked exactly the same. Had anything happened to me? I looked at the clock. It was nearly half-past three! I had been away from my time for more than five hours! I had travelled in time!

I took a deep breath. I decided to use only the starting lever. Before I could change my mind, I pressed it with both hands. At once, my laboratory grew faint and hazy until it disappeared altogether. I suppose it must have been destroyed in the future. Now I was in the open air, on this hillside where my house stands now.

Day came, then night, then day again…days and nights, one after the other, faster and faster. Tall buildings rose up in front of my eyes. A strange noise filled my ears. It is difficult to describe the feelings of time travel, but they are very unpleasant. I felt helpless as I plunged forward. Night followed day like the flapping of a black wing.

I saw the moon spinning from new to full, and glimpsed the stars. Faster and faster…night and day merged into one. I saw trees growing, then dying. The surface of the earth seemed to melt and flow. The seasons flashed before me, until this hillside grew greener and there was no winter.

I felt that I was going mad, but I did not want to stop. The Time Machine began to sway and shudder and I seemed to be falling. Anxious thoughts began to fill my head. Would I be able to stop my machine? And if I did, would I be blown to pieces?

At that moment, I decided to press the stopping lever. With a noise like thunder, the Time Machine turned over and flung me into the air. I opened my eyes, eager to read the dials on my machine.

"It's the year Eight Hundred and Two Thousand Seven Hundred and One AD!" I gasped.

Trembling, I looked around me. I was sitting on a lawn, next to my overturned machine. Thick hail started to fall and, at first, I could only see bright purple flowers. Then, as the hail thinned, I saw an enormous white marble statue on a bronze pedestal at the end of the garden. This statue had huge, hovering wings and its

sightless eyes seemed to watch me. There was a faint smile on its lips.

The sun came out as I stood staring at the wooded hillside, and at the strange tall buildings in the distance. Then I looked again at that white statue. Suddenly, I was filled with terror at what I had done. What if human beings had become cruel and inhuman? What if I seemed like a savage animal to them? What if they wanted to kill me?

I was full of fear and panic. I pulled the Time Machine back onto its legs. I felt like a small bird in the air, knowing that a hawk above might swoop at any minute and kill it. With each second, my fear became greater. I put out my hand towards the starting lever.

I wanted to go back to my own world.

CHAPTER THREE

The little people

But I did not press the lever. Suddenly, my courage came back. I wanted to look more closely at this future world.

Not far away, I saw a group of people dressed in soft robes, whispering and looking across at me. They started to run across the lawn. The first one to reach me was a small man – about four feet high – wearing a purple tunic held by a leather belt. His legs were bare and he wore sandals. He seemed a beautiful and graceful creature, but very frail.

I took my hands from the Time Machine and in another moment, we were standing face to face – I and this fragile creature of the future.

The man laughed and I was amazed that he was not more afraid. He turned to the two others who had followed him and spoke to them in a very strange and sweet-sounding language. Others came until there were about eight or ten people around me. One of them spoke to me. I shook my head, pointed to my ears, and shook my head again. He hesitated, then touched my hand. They all began to touch me, to make sure that I was real. These pretty, child-like creatures did not frighten me at all. And they looked so frail that I felt that I could have easily knocked them over. I was even afraid that my voice would be too harsh for them.

They began to touch the Time Machine. I quickly reached over and unscrewed the little starting lever, and put it in my pocket.

I looked at the little people more closely. Each one had curly hair and tiny ears. Their mouths were small with bright red, thin lips, and their little chins were pointed. Their eyes were large and gentle, and did not seem to show much interest. They made no effort to speak to me again. They stood round me, smiling and speaking softly to each other.

I tried to find a way of talking about time. I pointed to the Time Machine, then I pointed to the sun. At once, a pretty little creature dressed in purple and white imitated the sound of thunder. She thought I had come from the sun in a thunderstorm! The thought came to me - were these creatures fools? I was in the year Eight Hundred and Two Thousand Seven Hundred and One! I expected people to be far ahead of us in knowledge. I was disappointed. Had I wasted my time, building the Time Machine?

I just nodded and made a loud noise like a clap of thunder. They jumped, and stepped back from me. Then one of the creatures placed a chain of flowers around my neck and they all laughed and clapped. They ran to bring more flowers and threw them at me until I was almost buried under them.

Then the little people began to pull me towards an enormous grey stone building. I left the Time Machine on the grass among the flowers and went with them.

How dingy I looked in my dark, nineteenth-century clothes! I entered the building, surrounded by a mass of soft robes and shining white limbs and laughter.

The first room inside was full of tables, slabs of polished stone raised from the floor. The tables were piled high with strange fruits. We all sat down on cushions between the tables. The little people began to eat the fruit with their hands, flinging peel and stalks into the openings in the sides of the tables. I did the same because I was hungry and thirsty.

I was amazed at the shabbiness of the building. Its stained-glass windows were broken in many places, and their curtains were thick with dust. But everybody seemed happy. About two hundred people watched me, their eyes shining as they ate. I learned later that they ate only fruit. Horses, cattle and sheep had all become extinct. And they did not have fire or light or matches…"

"But I am going ahead in my story," the Time Traveller smiled. "Let me go back to that first day…"

"I must learn the speech of these new people," I thought. "I shall start now."

I held up a piece of fruit and pointed to it. They stared at me in surprise and laughed. Then a fair-haired little creature repeated a name. They chattered for a long time to each other about it. I said the word. They laughed. I felt like a school master with my pupils. In this way, I learned many names. But it was slow work, and the creatures soon grew tired of it.

"They are not interested for long," I thought. "They are like small children who wander away to find a new toy. I can see little difference between the men, the women and the children."

I left the great hall because I wanted to see the sunset. For the first time, the little people did not follow me. I saw that the grey building was on the slope of a wide river valley, as if the River Thames had moved about a mile from where it is today. I decided to climb one of the hills in the distance to look down on the valley.

"There are no fences, no hedges, no houses," I thought, "only palaces and one big garden. Perhaps they all live together, like some people do in my world."

I stared at the purple and crimson horizon, and thought about the fragile people I had met.

"They seem so weak," I thought. "My people in the nineteenth-century are strong because we have to work hard. We have to find out what causes disease, how to improve our crops and our animals. Our aim in life is to make everybody happy and healthy. But these people are healthy, happy and secure. They dance and sing in the sunlight and pick flowers. They have no aim in life and it has made them weak."

As I stood there in the growing darkness, I was pleased that I had answered all my questions about this strange new world. A full moon came out and I shivered with the cold.

"I must go back and find somewhere to sleep," I thought.

As I looked for the grey building, I caught sight of the white marble statue in the bright moonlight. I could see the flowers, black in the pale light, and the little lawn. I looked at the lawn again and my blood ran cold.

I could not see the Time Machine.

CHAPTER FOUR

Where is the Time Machine?

I could hardly breathe and my throat tightened.

"What if I am left here for ever?" I asked myself, trembling violently.

I ran all the way down the hill. I fell and cut my face, but I got up and ran on, blood trickling down my cheek and chin. I covered the distance of about two miles in ten minutes – and I am not a young man!

"They must have moved it!" I said over and over again. "They have pushed it under the bushes out of the way. Why, oh why did I leave my machine? Why?"

When I reached the lawn, I saw that my worst fears had come true. The Time Machine had gone. I looked at the empty space and felt faint and cold. Above me, the white shining face of the statue seemed to laugh at me.

"It cannot have moved in time," I said to cheer myself up, "The starting lever is in my pocket. But where is it?"

I ran in and out of the bushes. Not a creature moved in that moonlit world. Then, sobbing, I went up to the grey building. The hall was dark, silent and deserted. I walked through it to a second hall where the floor was covered with cushions. About twenty little people were sleeping on them.

"Where is my Time Machine?" I shouted like an angry child. I shook some of them. A few of them laughed but most of them were frightened. I ran outside again – like a strange animal in an unknown world. At last, I lay down next to the statue and wept. Then I went to sleep.

In the morning, I felt calmer.

"I behaved very badly last night," I told myself. "What if the Time Machine is lost? I can always build another one. But I am sure it has only been taken away. I must be patient and find it."

As I got up, I noticed some marks on the grass, and strange footprints next to them. They led from the spot where I had left the Time Machine to the bronze pedestal next to me. I tapped it with my fingers.

"It's hollow!" I whispered. "I am sure that my Time Machine is inside. But there are no handles. How can I get in?"

A man hurried past the statue. I pointed to the pedestal and tried to ask him how to open it, but he carried on walking. I caught him angrily by the end of his robe and dragged him towards it. The poor creature looked so horrified that I let him go.

"I'll fetch a big pebble from the river and break down the doors," I decided.

I hammered on the bronze for a long time, but I could

not break it. The little people must have heard me, but nobody came to see what I was doing. At last, hot and tired, I sat down.

"You have to be patient," I told myself. "If they want to steal my machine, they will, and there is no point in destroying the bronze panels. If they don't intend to steal it, I will get it back as soon as I can learn to ask for it. I must try to understand the ways of this future world."

Suddenly, I laughed out loud. I had spent years trying to get into the future. Now I wanted to escape from it!

I decided to work harder at learning the language, so that I could ask them where the Time Machine was. To my surprise, their language was extremely simple. There were only one or two words in each sentence. It was impossible to talk about ideas or to ask anything complicated. However, I did learn that these beautiful little people were called the Eloi.

I wanted to explore further, but I dared not go far from my point of arrival. As far as I could see, the land beyond the Thames valley was covered with blossom-laden trees, and thick bushes, and here and there the water shone like silver. There were beautiful buildings everywhere.

I began to notice that there were many wells sunk into the ground, with tall towers next to them. I found one of them on the hill I had climbed that first evening. I peered down into the darkness, but I could not see any water.

I felt in my pocket, hoping to find the box of matches I usually carried with me. I took out a match and leaned over the well. When I lit it, there was no reflection of the flame. But I could hear a noise…THUD! THUD! THUD! …like the beating of a big engine. Was there air down there? I threw down a piece of paper.

"I thought it would flutter down slowly," I murmured, "but it has been sucked away quickly. Perhaps these are the water drains for the Eloi."

How wrong I was!

CHAPTER FIVE

A friend at last

On my third day with the Eloi, I woke up very early. I tried to go to sleep again, but I felt restless and uncomfortable. It was that strange time of the day when everything seems grey and unreal. I left the palace to watch the sunrise. The moon was setting, turning the bushes inky-black in the half-light. The ground and the sky were grey. I looked up at the hill.

"I can see white shapes running up the hill!" I gasped. "And they are carrying something, I'm sure! Are they ghosts? Now they've vanished. Perhaps it was a trick of the light!"

I thought about those white creatures all morning, sitting by the water where the little people were bathing. Suddenly, one of them cried out in pain, as if it had cramp, and was carried away by the river. Not one of those people tried to save the little person, crying weakly as it drowned. I quickly waded into the water and caught the poor thing, and brought it back to land.

The next morning, this little woman – I believe that's what she was – brought me a garland of flowers. We sat down and smiled, and gave each other flowers, and she kissed my hands. Then I tried to talk.

"What is your name?" I asked in her language.

"Weena."

That was the beginning of our strange and short friendship.

Weena was like a child. She wanted to be with me all the time. She tried to follow me everywhere, but she got too tired. If I left her, she became upset and clung to me. I did not know until later the real cause of her distress when I left her alone. Then it was too late.

"So there is still fear in the world," I thought to myself. "I have also noticed that Weena is terrified of the dark. All these people are. As soon as the sun goes down, they go inside. They are never outside after dark, and they never sleep alone. But why?"

For the five nights of our friendship, Weena overcame some of her fear and slept with her head on my arm, away from the other Eloi.

The weather was much hotter on this future earth. On the fourth morning after my arrival, I was wandering alone near a ruin in the hot sun. I decided to go inside where it was dark and cool. Suddenly, I stopped. A pair of eyes was watching me out of the darkness. I was afraid to turn back, in case a wild beast jumped on me. I made myself walk forward and put out my hand. I touched something soft. At once, the eyes darted sideways and a white shape ran past me.

I turned to look, my heart in my mouth. A strange, ape-like creature, its head held down, ran past me. It was white, with large grey-red eyes, and yellow hair on its head and back. It staggered, then disappeared behind another pile of rocks.

I went over to the rocks. I could not find it at first. Then I came across one of the wells. Had the creature escaped down there? I lit a match and held it over the opening. There it was - a small, white moving creature, which stared back at me. I shuddered.

"It's climbing down the wall!" I gasped. "It's like a human spider!"

I do not know how long I sat staring into the well.

"It was a human being!" I whispered at last. "Now I understand. There are two kinds of creatures on earth now – the beautiful creatures of the Upper-world, the Eloi – and this terrible white creature that lives only in the dark, inside the earth. But why are there two sorts of humans? I must go down there and find out."

But I was too afraid.

CHAPTER SIX

The Morlocks

I sat for a long time and tried to work out the answer to my question. In the time that I had been in the future, I had seen no shops, no workshops, no machinery of any kind. The little people did not work. What if these creatures – the Undergrounders - did all the work? After all, in our world today, we try to put the working parts underground – our trains, and mines, even workrooms. Poor people often work in terrible factories shut off from the light. And at the same time, rich people own a great deal of land and live a life of pleasure.

I could see for myself that the Eloi – the Uppergrounders – now lived only for pleasure and were losing their intelligence and strength. But what was happening to the creatures underground? Suddenly, a terrible thought came into my mind. Had they hidden my Time Machine under the statue?

"I want to go underground and find out," I thought. "But I am still afraid."

I walked away from the well and found Weena.

"Who are those creatures down there?" I asked her. She refused to answer.

"Tell me," I said more angrily. "I must know."

Weena burst into tears.

"Morlocks," she whispered at last.

They were the only tears I ever saw in the future, apart from my own. I could not bear to see Weena cry. I lit a match, knowing that this would please her, and soon she was smiling and clapping her hands again.

I wanted to see the Morlocks so much! Only my fear stopped me. I was so restless that I wandered further and further from the stone building, towards the south-west where Wimbledon stands today. I caught sight of an enormous green building in the distance, shining as if it was made of porcelain. I called it the Palace of Green Porcelain from then on, and I wanted to go closer.

"No, I am just putting off my visit to the Morlocks," I told myself firmly. "Be brave! Go down there and find out what has happened to the Time Machine. They are afraid of the light and you have a few matches left."

Early the next morning, I forced myself to go back to one of the wells. Weena came with me, dancing all the way. But when I peered into the well, she looked upset. I lifted her up to kiss her, then put her down again.

"Goodbye, little Weena," I said.

I leaned over and felt for the foot hold at the top of the well. Weena gave the most terrible cry I have ever heard and pulled me back with her little hands. I pushed her away and climbed into the well. As I went down, it

grew darker and the thudding of the machines below me became louder. At last, I came to a small tunnel at the bottom of the well where I rested for a while.

Suddenly, a soft hand touched my face. I sat up quickly and picked up my box of matches. I lit a match. In front of me were three stooping white creatures, like the one

I had seen in the ruins. They ran away from the light, vanishing into the tunnels. From there, they glared at me with their huge eyes.

I felt my way along the wall of the tunnel, and soon I came to a large open cave. I struck another match and shadowy Morlocks ran to hide from its glare. I walked forward and sniffed.

"Blood!" I gasped.

I caught sight of a little table of white metal, set for a meal.

"At least they eat meat!" I thought. "But what large animal have they killed? There are no animals above the ground!"

I had only four matches left so I stood in the dark for a while. A hand touched mine and smelly fingers ran over my face, then my body.

"Go away!" I shouted.

They scuttled into the darkness, then came back again. They caught hold of me and I shouted again. They made a noise like laughter. I was so terrified that I lit another match and ran towards the bottom of the well. But the air blew out my match.

I could hear the Morlocks in the darkness, rustling like wind among leaves, and pattering like rain, as they hurried after me. Then I felt their hands pulling me back.

CHAPTER SEVEN

The Palace of Green Porcelain

Terrified, I struck a match and waved it at the Morlocks. I stared in horror at their dazzled faces – those pale, chinless faces and huge, lidless, pinkish-grey eyes! I did not stay to look for very long. I ran on, striking a second match, then a third. At last, I came to the bottom of the well. I stopped, feeling for the bottom rung of the ladder, and the Morlocks tugged at me violently. I lit my last match, but it fizzled out.

I kicked the Morlocks away and put my foot onto the first rung. I only just managed to hold on. One Morlock followed me, but I kicked it away. I scrambled up the side of the well, and when I reached the top I fell down on the ground. I remember Weena kissing my hands and ears, and the voices of the other Eloi. Then I fainted.

When I came round again, I was in despair.

"Oh why did I go down to see the Morlocks?" I cried. "They will think that I have declared war on them! They will come after me! If only I had not used up all my matches! How can I ask them to give me back my Time Machine now?"

And I had another enemy – which surprised me, and will surprise you – the dark. At last I understood the fear

that the Eloi had of the dark. It was the time when the Morlocks came. But what did they come for? Suddenly, I remembered their meat. It had looked familiar, but I did not know why.

"I am not going to be afraid of the Morlocks," I thought. "I am not like the helpless little Eloi. In my century, we do not let fear take us over. I shall fight back, not hide away in fear. I shall find a safe place to sleep tonight, then I shall look for weapons to defend myself. Then I shall be ready to face them."

I wandered all day along the valley of the Thames, looking for such a place. But all the buildings and hills could easily be climbed by the Morlocks. Then I remembered the Palace of Green Porcelain, high on a hill in South London. Perhaps there would be no Morlocks there. I decided to go. I put Weena on my shoulders and set off. After a while, she got down and ran beside me, picking flowers to put in my pockets…"

The Time Traveller stopped speaking for a moment and put his hand in his pocket. He took out two large, white withered flowers and put them on the table without speaking. Then he started his story again…

"It was much further than I had thought and the sun was setting as we saw the walls of the palace in the distance. Weena pointed to the grey stone building down below us and began to cry.

"No, Weena," I said, "we can't go back now. We shall be safe in the Palace of Green Porcelain."

We walked on in silence. As the sky darkened, Weena became more afraid. I carried her again and she pressed her face against my shoulder. From the top of the next hill, I saw a thick wood spreading in front of us, wide and dark. I hesitated. Were the Morlocks already hiding in the trees, waiting for us?

"We shall have to spend the night on the hill," I thought, "it will be safer. If only I had some matches!

They would have kept the Morlocks away."

I wrapped Weena in my jacket and sat next to her, waiting for the moon to rise. The night was very clear and the stars made me feel safe for a moment. Then I shivered. Man as I knew him no longer existed in this future. Instead there were these frail creatures and the white monsters that terrified me and the Eloi. I looked at the sleeping Weena. Then I realised. The meat I had seen on the table was an Eloi!

The Morlocks did not come in the night and, in the pink dawn, I felt almost happy again. We went down into the wood and found fruit for our breakfast. We laughed and danced in the sunlight. Then I thought again of the Morlock's meat again. From the bottom of my heart, I pitied the Eloi – they were no more than fatted cattle. I turned my thoughts back to how I could help myself and little Weena.

"I must get to the green palace quickly," I told myself. "I'm sure that I can find weapons there. Then I can go back and break down the bronze doors. I know the Time Machine is in there. I must get away from here as soon as possible."

But what would happen to Weena?

"I will take her back to my world," I decided.

CHAPTER EIGHT

Terror in the woods

We did not reach the Palace of Green Porcelain until midday. As we walked through its dusty and deserted galleries, we found dinosaur skeletons, fossils, stuffed animals, old books, weapons and enormous machines. The longest gallery was dark at the end, and I saw small narrow footprints in the dust. Down in that blackness, I heard a pattering sound and the same strange noises I had heard down the well.

"It is late in the afternoon and I still have no light and no weapons!" I cried. "We must get back before dark!"

I reached up to one of the machines and pulled off a metal lever.

"This will crush a Morlock skull," I thought. "How I long to kill one of them!"

The Time Traveller looked at us strangely for a moment.

"You may think it cruel of me, gentlemen, to want to kill one of our descendants; but I had no feelings for them at all!"

Then he carried on with his story.

"As we were leaving the palace, I saw something which filled me with joy – a box of matches in an

36

airtight case! They were not even damp."

"Dance, Weena!" I shouted with delight. "Now we have a weapon against these horrible creatures! We do not need to find a hiding-place now. I have the best weapon of all against the Morlocks – matches!"

And there in that derelict museum, among the thick dust, I whistled and sang.

"We will set off for the grey palace now," I told Weena. "We can sleep safely in the open air tonight. I will light a fire to keep the Morlocks away. And in the morning, I can break down the bronze pedestal and find the Time Machine."

We set off when the sun was just sinking below the horizon. But we travelled slowly because I was tired and I had to carry Weena. It was dark when we reached the wood. We should not have gone into it, but I wanted to carry on to the bare hill on the other side. It was safer there.

I hesitated, afraid. Then I caught sight of three crouching Morlocks in the black bushes around us. We were surrounded by long grass and I was sure that the creatures would creep up on us, unseen.

"We will go on through the wood," I decided. "I can set fire to some of the bushes behind us. It will show us the way and stop the Morlocks from following us."

If only I had stopped to think how dangerous and

stupid this was! But I thought only of escaping from the Morlocks. I lit a small fire. Weena, like all the other Eloi, had never seen a fire before. She wanted to run into it and play with it. I pulled her away and we set off through the wood. The fire lit our way for a while, then the wood became dark again. I could not strike any more matches as I had to carry Weena in one arm, and my metal lever in the other.

At first, I heard only the sound of twigs crackling under my feet and the faint rustle of the breeze above me. Later, I heard a pattering noise near me, which grew louder. Then I heard the same sounds and voices I had heard underground.

I knew now that there were more Morlocks in the wood – and they were coming closer.

CHAPTER NINE
Death by fire

In another moment, I felt a tug at my coat and something touched my arm. Weena shivered violently and became very still. I had to light a match so I put her on the ground. Soft, creeping hands touched my coat and my back, even my neck. The match blazed and I saw the white backs of the Morlocks as they ran away from its light. Then I looked at Weena. She was lying still at my feet, her face to the ground, hardly breathing.

I quickly lit some wood and flung it blazing, to the ground. The Morlocks ran back to the shadows. I knelt down and lifted Weena up and put her over my shoulder. I set off again. But now I had no idea which way I was facing.

"What if I am walking back towards the green palace?" I thought, trembling. "I'll build a fire and stay here until morning."

I put Weena onto the ground and began to collect sticks and leaves. I caught sight of the Morlocks' eyes shining in the darkness. I had to light a match quickly when two white shapes came closer. Weena, terrified, ran away. One Morlock, blinded by the light, walked straight into me. I hit it hard and I felt its bones grind under my fist. Weena came back and lay down again, next to my lever, as I lit the fire.

If only I had not fallen asleep, I could have saved Weena. But my eyes closed slowly as I sat by the warmth of the fire. And when I opened them, the fire had gone out. There were Morlocks everywhere, touching me in the dark. I quickly put my hand into my pocket for the box of matches. Where was it? I felt again. But, like Weena, it had disappeared!

The creatures pulled me down by the neck, by the hair, by the arms until they covered me.

Their teeth nipped my neck.

"Help! Help!" I cried, "I am in a giant spider's web!"

Fighting them with all my strength, I managed to roll over and reach the lever. I struggled to my feet, shaking the human rats from me, and hitting their faces. For a moment, I was free of them. I stood with my back to a tree, swinging the lever in front of me.

The wood was filled with the sound of their cries, but they did not come near. Then, to my amazement, I saw that they were running away from me. Their backs seemed no longer white, but reddish. Why were they so afraid?

As I stared after them, I saw little red sparks shooting between the branches of the trees. At last I understood the smell of burning wood, the red glow and the Morlocks' flight. The wood was on fire! I looked for Weena, but the fire crackled loudly as each new tree burst into flames. Gripping my lever, I had to follow the Morlocks out of the wood.

And then I saw the most horrible thing I had seen since I had arrived in the future. I came to a small open space surrounded by fire. In the middle of this space was a small hill, full of Morlocks - thirty or forty of them - dazzled by the light and the heat of the fire. They ran everywhere in their panic, unable to see. I did not need to hit any more of them. I even walked on the hill among them, looking for Weena. But Weena was gone.

"They must have left her poor little body in the wood when they ran away," I wept, "and now she has burned to death. Poor little Weena! But it is better than becoming Morlock meat. How I wish I could kill every one of these terrible creatures!"

At last, I sat at the top of the hill and watched this strange group of blind creatures, groping their way and making strange sounds to each other in the glare of the fire. Most of that night seemed like a nightmare. I bit myself and screamed, and beat the ground with my hands.

"Please, God, let me wake up!" I cried over and over again.

Some of the Morlocks rushed into the flames as they tried to escape, holding their heads down away from the brightness of the fire. Then, slowly, the flames died down and black smoke rose into the air. At last, dawn came. I stood up and, through the smoke, I could see the Palace of Green Porcelain. From that, I knew which direction to take.

A few surviving Morlocks scurried away as the day grew clearer. I tied some grass around my feet and limped through the smoking ashes towards the hiding-place of my Time Machine…"

The Time Traveller stopped speaking for a moment. Then he spoke quietly.

"I could not believe that Weena was dead!" he whispered. "Now I was alone again, so alone. I began to think of this house and you, my friends."

We dared not speak, and he went on with his story.

"As I walked, I discovered, to my great joy, some loose matches in my pocket. About eight or nine o' clock in the morning, I came to the same hill I had climbed on my arrival. I looked down on the beauty below me, but now I knew what ugliness it hid.

"How sad that the world has come to this!" I thought sadly, "I expected so much more."

I slept for a long time, then I walked on to the white statue. To my surprise, the bronze doors of the pedestal were already open.

"The Morlocks must be in there, waiting for me!" I thought.

I stepped inside. In the corner stood the Time Machine. Suddenly, with a loud clang, the bronze panels closed behind me and I was in the dark.

"They think I am trapped," I laughed to myself, "they do not know I still have some matches and the starting lever in my pocket!"

But I had forgotten one thing. My matches would only light on the side of their box. They would not strike. My calm vanished. The little beasts were close to me, and one of them touched me. As I tried to fix one the starting levers into place, a Morlock snatched it from my hand. I was in greater danger then than I had been in the wood. I hit the beast with my head and cracked its skull. Then I picked up the lever and put it into place.

It wasn't a moment too soon. I pressed the lever. The clinging hands slipped from me, and a grey light took the place of the darkness.

And so I came back from the future.

CHAPTER TEN

Back to the present

The Time Traveller stopped speaking and looked at us.

"I know that all this will sound absolutely incredible to you," he sighed.

Nobody moved. Then the newspaper Editor stood up and put his hand on the Time Traveller's shoulder.

"What a pity you are not a writer of stories," he said.

"You don't believe it? I thought not," the Time Traveller said, "I hardly believe it myself."

"May I have these flowers?" the Doctor asked. "I should like to find out what they are."

"Certainly not," the Time Traveller said.

"Where did you really get them?" the Doctor asked.

The Time Traveller put his hand to his head.

"Weena put them in my pocket when I travelled into time," he said quietly. He started to walk towards the door. "I must look at my Time Machine again and make sure that I did not dream it!"

The Time Traveller picked up a lamp and rushed down the corridor to his laboratory. We followed him. There, in the flickering light of the lamp stood the Time Machine – smeared with moss and grass. He put down the lamp and turned to us.

"The story I told you was true," he said.

We left after that. I did not know whether I believed the story or not. But I decided to visit the Time Traveller again the next day. I found his laboratory empty. I stared for a minute at the Time Machine, put out my hand and touched the lever. As I was going back to the house, I met the Time Traveller in the corridor, carrying a rucksack and a camera.

"I'm very busy," he said quickly.

"Did you really travel through time?" I asked.

"Yes, I did," he answered.

He looked straight at me.

"I know why you have come," he said. "Stay here for half-an-hour and I'll prove to you that time-travelling is real. Yes, stay, we'll have lunch in half-an-hour, and I can tell you where I have been. Then perhaps you will believe me."

I nodded. Then he closed the door of his laboratory. I remembered that I had to meet a friend at two o'clock, and I ran after the Time Traveller to tell him. I took hold of the handle of the door. A strange noise was coming from the room - THUD! CLICK! As I opened the door, I heard the sound of glass breaking on the floor.

The Time Traveller was not there.

Just for a moment, I thought I saw a ghostly figure sitting in a whirling mass of black and brass. But this ghostly sight vanished as I rubbed my eyes. I looked up and saw that the skylight of the laboratory was broken.

Then I noticed that the Time Machine had gone.

I stayed there for a while, waiting for the Time Traveller to come back, waiting for another story and the photographs he would bring with him. But as I write this, I am beginning to fear that I shall have to wait for the rest of my life. All I have to remind me of him are two strange, white withered flowers.

The Time Traveller vanished three years ago. And, as everyone knows now, he has never returned.